For Rana Esculenta

and with thanks to my two guinea-pigs,
Rose and Albert

asserted.

Rockwell.

Data is available.

978-1-4063-0981-2

www.walkerbooks.co.uk

BEWARE OF THE FROG

william bee

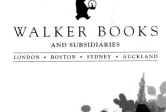

WALKER BOOKS
AND SUBSIDIARIES
LONDON · BOSTON · SYDNEY · AUCKLAND

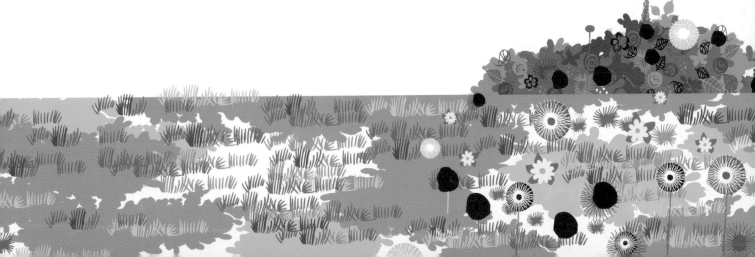

This is the story
of a sweet little old lady
called Mrs Collywobbles.

Mrs Collywobbles lives in
a little house on the edge of
a big dark scary wood.

The only thing protecting
Mrs Collywobbles from all
the horrible creatures that live
in the big dark scary wood is ...

her little pet frog.

Look! There is little Mrs Collywobbles
hiding in her kitchen.
Who has she seen coming
out of the big dark scary wood?

Oh dear!
It's that terrible thief,
Greedy Goblin, up to
no good – out stealing from
sweet little old ladies.

"Nickerty-noo, Nickerty-noo,
if I get a chance,
I'll steal from you...

I love to steal money
and shiny pretty things...
I'm in and out of the house
in a flash."

"What's this ... **'BEWARE OF THE FROG'**?
Well, no frog will stop me getting what
I want. Maybe I'll just steal that frog too!

Nickerty-noo, Nickerty-noo,
if I get a chance,
I'll steal from you..."

And so Greedy Goblin quietly
opens the gate.

But, oh dear, the frog doesn't
look very pleased about that...

Look! There is little Mrs Collywobbles
hiding in her bathroom.
Who has she seen coming
out of the big dark scary wood?

Oh dear!

It's Smelly Troll, up to no good.
He moves into little old ladies'
houses and pongs so much
they have to run away...

"*Welly-welly, Welly-welly,*
I'm awfully slimy
and awfully smelly...

This little old lady's house is
just what I've been looking for...
I'll whiff something rotten
so she'll soon run away."

"What's this ... **'BEWARE OF THE FROG'**?
I'll belch and whiff and stink so much,
that frog will have to hop off too!

Welly-welly, Welly-welly,
I'm awfully slimy
and awfully smelly..."

And so, with a pong,
Smelly Troll opens the gate.

But, oh dear, the frog doesn't
look very pleased about that...

Look! There is little Mrs Collywobbles
hiding in her bedroom.
Who has she seen coming
out of the big dark scary wood?

Oh dear! Oh dear!
It's Giant Hungry Ogre!
He's after his supper
and his favourite food is ...
sweet little old lady.

"*Dum-de-dum, Dum-de-dum,*
I've got a very very hungry tum.

This looks promising ...
my belly's rumbling and
I must have my supper.
A juicy old lady
cooked in lots of
honey and butter."

"What's this ... **'BEWARE OF THE FROG'**?
Yum yum, that frog will taste lovely
dipped in some ketchup.

Dum-de-dum, Dum-de-dum,
I've got a very very hungry tum."

And so Giant Hungry Ogre
licks his lips and opens the gate.

But, oh dear, the frog doesn't
look very pleased about that...

So that was the story of a sweet
little old lady called Mrs Collywobbles,
who lived next to a big dark scary wood.

And as you can see Mrs Collywobbles
no longer has to spend all her time hiding
in her little house. And it's all thanks to ...

her little pet frog.

"Oh, my little froggy friend,
how can I ever thank you?"
asks Mrs Collywobbles.

The frog has a think...

"How about a little kiss?"
suggests the frog.
So Mrs Collywobbles
gives him a little kiss ... and ...

HEY PRESTO!

Mrs Collywobbles is transformed
into a sweet little old lady ... frog.

But, oh dear, she doesn't look
very pleased about that ...

... does she?